Pumpkin Baby

To my little pumpkin baby brother, Steve Yolen, and all his grandbabies. — J.Y.

For Ewan, who will always be my little pumpkin. — S.M.

Library and Archives Canada in Publication information available upon request

The publisher gratefully acknowledges the support of the Canada Council for the Arts and the Ontario Arts Council for its publishing program. We acknowledge the support of the Government of Ontario through the Ontario Media Development Corporation's Ontario Book Initiative.

We acknowledge the financial support of the Government of Canada through the Book Publishing Industry Development Program (BPIDP) for our publishing activities.

KPk is an imprint of
Key Porter Books Limited
Six Adelaide Street East, Tenth Floor
Toronto, Ontario
Canada M5C 1H6

Design: Marijke Friesen

Printed and bound in China

09 10 11 12 13 5 4 3 2 1

Pumpkin Baby

written by

Jane Yolen

illustrated by

Susan Mitchell

KPk
Key Porter Kids

When I was three years old,
old enough to know better,

Mama took a ripe pumpkin
from Auntie May's patch of land.

Auntie May called out,
hoe in hand,
"Gonna get a baby that way
from all those seeds.
A pumpkin baby."

Their laughter flew back and forth,
back and forth, across the rows.

I thought about a pumpkin baby.
Would it be orange on the outside?
Would it be too heavy to pick up,
too round to run and play with me?
Would I,
   could I,
      ever love a pumpkin child?

When I was four years old,
old enough to know much better,

Mama gathered a plump green cabbage
from Auntie May's patch of land.

"Gonna find a baby in that cabbage patch,"
Mr. Jess called from his porch,
"a cabbage baby."

Their laughter flew back and forth,
back and forth, across the rich tilled soil.

I thought about a cabbage baby.
Would it have leafy green cheeks?
Would it stand in long, straight rows,
its tiny cabbage feet tucked into dirt?
Would I,
   could I,
      ever love a cabbage child?

When I was five years old,
old enough to know much
    much better,
a big stork flew overhead,
its long legs trailing.

"Gonna drop a baby down your chimney,"
Mr. Thompson said, delivering our mail.
"A stork baby, doncha know."

Mama grabbed the mail and their laughter
flew back and forth, back and forth,
across the road.

I thought about a stork baby.
Would it fly up
from the changing table,
wet diapers around
its long baby legs?
Would I,
could I,
ever love a stork child?

Now I'm six years old,
old enough to know much much much better.

When our new baby was born,
he was not orange-coloured like a pumpkin,
but was way too heavy for me to pick up
without Papa's help.

Mama says that soon enough
he will go from a pumpkin baby
to a cabbage baby,
his little cheeks soft as leaves
and full of smiles.

Soon enough he will go
from a cabbage baby
to a stork baby,

getting down from his changing table
on his long legs, to run after me.

If you are six years old,
you know that you
could love him,
would love him,
DID love him—
pumpkin,
cabbage,
stork baby—
from the very moment
    he was born.